THE STORY OF THE X-MEN

Adapted by Thomas Macri

Illustrated by Pat Olliffe and Hi-Fi Design

Based on the Marvel comic book series X-Men

MARVEL

New York • Los Angeles

marvelkids.com

© 2013 MARVEL

Printed in the United States of America

First Edition

1 3 5 7 9 10 8 6 4 2

G658-7729-4-13121

ISBN 978-1-4231-7224-6

Everyone is different.

But some people are very different.
They don't fit in with others.

They are born with powers.
They are called mutants!

Some people are afraid of mutants.
They are afraid of their powers.
They are scared of them because
they are different.
This fear makes these people mean.
It makes them angry.

They chase mutants away.
They don't want them around.

This is Charles Xavier. He is
a professor.
He calls himself Professor X.

NEWS UPDATE: MUTANTS ATTACK LIBE

Professor X dreams of
a better world.
In this world humans are nice
to mutants.

Professor X is a mutant.

He can read minds.

He wanted to use his gift to make his dream come true.

He needed to find other mutants who could help him, too.

He met Scott Summers. Scott could
shoot beams from his eyes. Professor X
called him Cyclops.

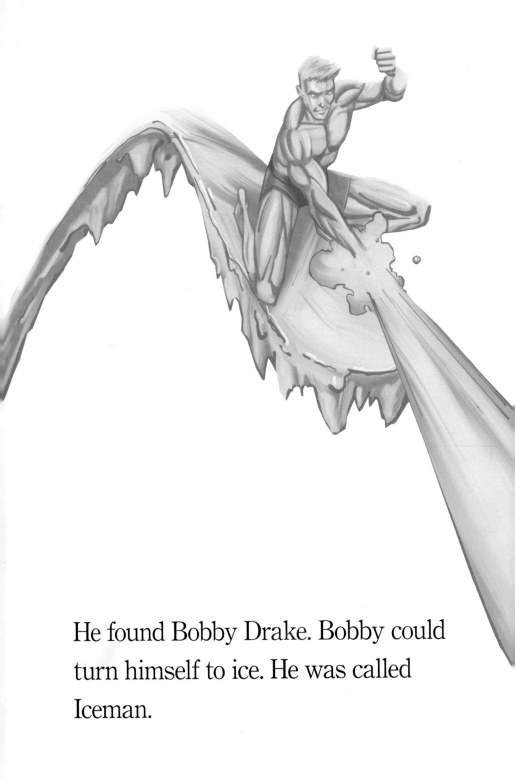

He found Bobby Drake. Bobby could
turn himself to ice. He was called
Iceman.

Next, the professor met
Warren Worthington.
Warren had wings like a bird's.
He could fly. He called himself Angel.

He also found Hank McCoy. Hank could
swing and jump. He was like an animal.
He called himself the Beast.

Jean Grey was the last mutant to
join the group. She could move things
with her mind. She was called Marvel Girl.

Together they formed a team.
They were called the X-Men.
They were going to fight
for Professor X's dream!

The X-Men's first battle was against
a man named Magneto. Magneto wanted
mutants to rule over humans.

The X-Men chased him away.

Magneto never gave up. He formed his own team called the Brotherhood.

They fought against the X-Men.

The X-Men needed to fight harder.
They soon grew in number.
Cyclops's brother Alex joined
the X-Men. He could blast energy
from his hands. He was called Havok.
His friend Lorna Dane also joined.
She could move metal. She called
herself Polaris.

Once, the X-Men rushed off to a
dangerous mission.
They disappeared!
Professor X needed to find new X-Men.
He searched a special map to find them.

The new team was soon in place!

Wolverine had sharp claws.
They could cut through anything.

Nightcrawler could hide in the dark.
He could move from place to place
just by thinking about it.

Ororo Munroe could control
the weather. She was known as Storm.

Peter Rasputin could turn to metal.
He called himself Colossus.

Sean Cassidy had a powerful scream.
He was called Banshee.

John Proudstar was strong. His code
name was Thunderbird.

And Shiro Yoshida could shoot
fire and fly. He was called Sunfire.

The new team rescued the old X-Men.
They fought together. They beat the
mutant that had trapped the old X-Men.

They returned home. The new X-Men joined the team.

They trained hard.
They became real Super Heroes.

They will never stop fighting for
the professor's dream.